The First Time You Smiled

(or was it just wind?)

HarperCollins*Publishers*

HarperCollins*Publishers*
1 London Bridge Street
London SE1 9GF

www.harpercollins.co.uk

HarperCollins*Publishers*
Macken House,
39/40 Mayor Street Upper,
Dublin 1, D01 C9W8, Ireland

First published by
HarperCollins*Publishers* 2022

3 5 7 9 10 8 6 4 2

A catalogue record of this book is
available from the British Library

ISBN 9780008526146

Printed and bound by PNB, Latvia

MIX
Paper | Supporting
responsible forestry
FSC™ C007454

This book is produced from
independently certified FSC™ paper to
ensure responsible forest management.

For more information visit:
www.harpercollins.co.uk/green

A BABY RECORD JOURNAL WITH <u>ATTITUDE</u>

The First Time You Smiled

(or was it just wind?)

CAT SIMS

HarperCollins*Publishers*

Dedication:

To my girls, Billie and Bo,
and my husband, Jimmy Sims.
I love the life we've built together.

Contents

Introduction

Parenting did not come easily to me. Let's start with that. Cards on the table, balls-out honesty. In fact, I pretty much screwed it up right from the start. Or so I thought.

The reality was, I was nailing it. And you are too. Whether you're still planning for the arrival of your baby, or you're in the thick of it … please know you're doing a good job. You may not be able to remember the last time you showered and every available surface in your house is straining under the weight of eleventy-billion muslins covered in questionable damp patches from a range of unknown bodily fluids, but trust me, you're doing great.

You see, no one really knows what they're doing when we start out on the journey of parenting. We tend to be so sleep-deprived that we can't see the 'you're-doing-a-bloody-awesome-job' wood for the 'what-the-fuck-is-this-fresh-new-hell' trees. For that reason, I want this book to be a map through those thorny trees to the other side where things have settled down a bit, you've figured a lot of this stuff out, you're wiping fewer butts, picking less Weetabix out of your hair and finding fewer rogue bogeys wiped on your back.

But, if you're anything like me, you may still be worried that you screwed it up at first. That's when you can come back to this book and read about all the cool, funny, heart-warming stuff you achieved as a parent … because you really did – it was just hard to see it when you were in it.

If you're hoping for a cutesy, pastel-hued book covered in rabbits and teddy bears then I fear you will be severely disappointed. If, however, sarcasm, poo-jokes and brutal honesty are more your bag then you've come to the right place because hell, when it comes to parenting, if you don't laugh, you'll probably be found crying in a corner, begging to be told when it's all over.

So, this book is all about helping you to record all the stuff you want to remember in a cool, non-twee, totally parent-centred book that you'll actually want to fill in and keep, and hand over to your kids when they're old enough to use swear words. It'll be a reminder to you that you were a legend in your own parenting right, even if you sometimes forgot to buy nappies and had to wrap them in a tea-towel and take them to Sainsbury's at 8pm at night (just me?) and yes, of course she did a massive turd in the tea-towel.

This book is part record, part therapy, part best friend, part LOLs and part reality check for the next generation. It's the book of truth, the book that tells the real story, a book that will keep you grounded in reality and, I hope, a book that you will forever be proud of because, whatever your story looks like, it starts right here with you and that is spectacular.

All the love,

P.S. People often ask me where my website name *Not So Smug Now* came from. Well, it's simple. Before I had a baby, I thought I knew what I was doing. I imagined exactly what it was going to be like and how I was going to slip into the role of the perfect mother effortlessly. Oh, how I can laugh now. Inevitably, it took about three days before I broke the dummy free from its plastic packaging, shoved it in the baby's mouth and bought a truckload more because, on balance, I felt that a dummy was less damaging than throwing the baby (that wouldn't stop crying) out of the window.*

*for legal reasons, that is, of course, a joke. Sort of.

Letter to Your Child

I wanted to include a quick note from me to your child that features in these pages. I know you won't say any of these things yourself (you're too modest), so I'm going to say them for you.

Dear

(insert name here)

You may already know this, but just in case you don't, the person or people who created this book and gave it to you are hands-down superheroes. Maybe you're about to have your own kids, maybe you're thinking about it, maybe it's not even on your radar yet or ever, but know this: being a parent is the hardest, dirtiest, stinkiest, most glorious job in the world bar none and wiping your butt for three years or so is just the start of it.

I hope this book serves to capture all those special memories for you, but I also hope it pulls back the curtain on everything your parents did to get you to where you are now. They didn't really sleep, they barely had time to shower, you didn't let them go for a wee on their own until you were about seven, maybe eight, and for the first 10 years, 7am counted as a lie in. All those things are part and parcel of parenting, and they were happy to do it (mostly), but that doesn't mean there weren't days they wished they could send you back in your original packaging and request a refund.

So, go give them a hug. Thank them, high-five them, make them a cuppa or pour them a stiff drink … whatever their love language is because you may be the protagonist of this book, but whoever gave this book to you is the real hero.

All the love,

Cat
x

How to Use This Book

You can use it however you like, to be honest. I'm not here to tell you what to do, but I designed it to be used like a journal. Something you can fill in as you go, look over at the end of each day, week or month (whatever works for you) to remind yourself what a bloody amazing job you're doing. However you choose to use it, I ask only this:

- When you're feeling like a crap parent, please pick it up and start reading. I want what I write in here to make you laugh, but what *you* write in here should make you proud AF.

- When your kid does something hilarious/amazing/disgusting, please pick this book up and record it. Those kinds of things will really bulk out your speech at their 18th or 21st.

- If you don't remember the exact time and date of their first smile or shit because you were too goddamn tired when they decided to have a magical moment at 3.54am, don't worry. Record what you can and approximates are also fine. This is not a test.

- Be 100 per cent honest. I promise you, even if you find the truth hard to write or if you worry about what people will think when they read it, you'll treasure it so much more if it's honest.

- It's designed to be handed down to your child when they are older, perhaps about to turn 18 or 21, or perhaps when they are thinking about having children or are about to have children of their own, but you don't have to. It can, of course, be yours to keep and treasure.

- Finally, too many baby books forget that families come in all sorts of shapes, sizes and colours. I've tried hard to make this book wholly inclusive. I've tried to avoid any defining phrases that assume

a family must look like the cis-hetero, 2.4-kids version that's tied in a pink or blue bow and wrapped up in a picket fence. I've made no assumptions that you or your partner were pregnant or gave birth. Where necessary, I've left spaces for you to fill in your appropriate 'firsts' to avoid forcing you into traditional Christian-based calendar events. If you want to document your baby's first Christmas – great – fill that in, but maybe you'd prefer Hanukkah, Eid or Divali? This is a book to make your own.

That being said, if there are any pages that are irrelevant to your experience please feel free to cut them out of the book! I apologise in advance if there are parts of this book that, for any reason, I haven't succeeded in making inclusive. I'm learning, and welcome any feedback for subsequent print runs.

1

The Calm before the Baby Storm

(Journey to Birth)

Before I actually had a baby, I believed they'd eat organic food I made from scratch, never have a dummy and only ever play with wooden toys. I'm not so smug now.

The mother I thought I would be.

The mother I actually am ...

Our Story

HOW YOU CAME TO BE OUR BABY ...

☐ Your mum and dad had sex and here we are

☐ Your mum and dad went through IVF and here we are

☐ Your mum and dad chose a wonderful surrogate and here we are

☐ Your mum and dad chose a wonderful surrogate and donor and here we are

☐ Your mum and dad chose you specially through adoption and here we are

☐ Your mum(s) went through IVF with a wonderful donor and here we are

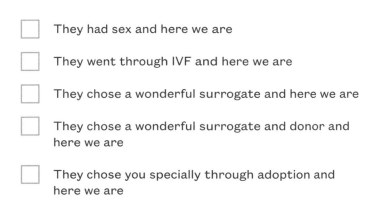

☐ Your mum(s) chose a wonderful surrogate and donor and here we are

☐ Your mum(s) chose you specially through adoption and here we are

☐ Your dad(s) chose a wonderful surrogate and here we are.

☐ Your dad(s) chose a wonderful surrogate and donor and here we are

☐ Your dad(s) chose you specially through adoption and here we are

☐ They had sex and here we are

☐ They went through IVF and here we are

☐ They chose a wonderful surrogate and here we are

☐ They chose a wonderful surrogate and donor and here we are

☐ They chose you specially through adoption and here we are

Our Story ...

Add in any and all the details you want to here.

Scan Pictures

Date: Hospital:

Weeks:

Anything else?

Date: Hospital:

Weeks:

Anything else?

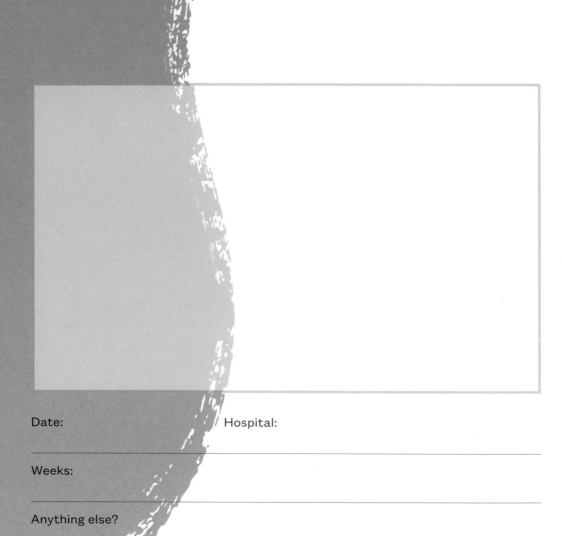

Date: _____   Hospital: _____

_____

Weeks: _____

_____

Anything else?

_____

_____

Date: Hospital:

_____

Weeks:

_____

Anything else?

_____

_____

If You Want Peace, You Must Prepare for War

There are heaps of lists available to help you get ready for having a baby. I don't know about you, but I found those slightly overwhelming, so I've tried to simplify it for you and boil it down to the bare necessities.

FOR THE BABY

- [ ] Something for it to sleep in

- [ ] Something to keep it warm at night

- [ ] Something to push it around in

- [ ] Something to put it down on when you actually need to use both your hands (a bouncer, bassinette etc.)

- [ ] Some stuff for it to wear: this does not include socks or any of those cute teeny-tiny shoes. They may look adorable but they are about as useful as a knitted condom and they'll stay on for 3.7 seconds if you're lucky (and no parent has ever been that lucky).

- [ ] Something for it to suck on: I know you think you won't use dummies and you might not (I didn't use a dummy with the first but I couldn't get a dummy in the second one quick enough) but it's worth having it there just in case. You don't want to be pacing at 4am with a screaming baby wishing you had a dummy to try, just in case that's the one thing that'll help.

- [ ] Something to carry it in (slings are excellent)

- [ ] Something to put it in the car in

- [ ] Something for it to eat: again, formula may not be on your list of things to do but, much like the dummy, it's good to have it there just in case. You may never use it but you don't want to be sending your partner to the 24-hour supermarket 30 miles away at 4am.

- [ ] Crisps, chocolate, a subscription to every streaming service available, Deliveroo app, a sign for the front door that reads, 'The baby is sleeping. Ring the bell and we will cut you,' a thermos mug that keeps your hot drinks hot, dry shampoo, eleventy-billion hair bobbles, a sleep mask, tracksuit bottoms and a bin for every room (trust me on this one).*

*This last one is a list for you, not the baby, obviously.

Every Picture Tells a Story

Some of you will have scan pictures. Some of you won't. This page is for you to stick any pictures, letters, notes or drawings that are part of your journey towards becoming parents.

Hacks and Advice

When you're expecting a baby, people love NOTHING MORE than offering you advice. From your relatives to your work colleagues to a stranger who stops you on the street: everyone has something to say to expectant parents.

A lot of the time, you'll smile sweetly and tell Aunty Janet how grateful you are even though you have no intention of leaving them in the buggy at the bottom of the garden with whisky rubbed on their gums when they don't stop crying (yes, this was legit advice an elderly relative gave me while I was pregnant).

But sometimes, occasionally, someone gives you some killer advice, a little golden nugget of parenting knowledge that you just want to shout from the rooftops and have tattooed on your forehead so that everyone you pass with a buggy can benefit from it (definitely don't do that). Other times, you'll be howling with laughter at the things that some people (dare to) say to you.

The funniest
thing someone said to me

This was said to me by

The most honest thing
someone told me

This was said to me by

The best piece
of advice I was given

This advice was
given to me by

The rudest thing
someone said to me

This was said to me by

29

2

Splash Down

(Birth)

Welcome to parenthood, where you'll add wipes, muslin cloths and dummies to the long list of 'things you can never find when you need them' and spend most of your time playing 'Guess the Bodily Fluid'.

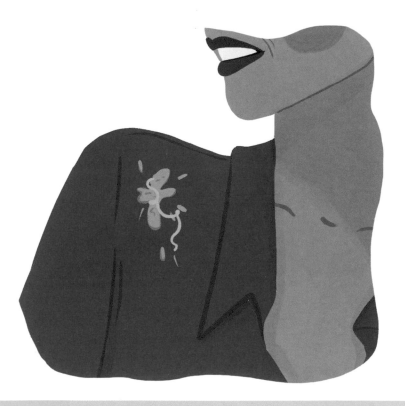

A Gut Reaction

However your baby arrives with you, knowing that your baby is coming can feel like a big GO button has been pushed. It's exciting and overwhelming but it can also be boring and long … really long. Here's a chance to record your feelings at that moment you discovered your baby's arrival was imminent. You can use different colour pens to record your reactions and your birth partner's reactions, if appropriate. I've also left a few blank spaces for you to get creative with. Tick all that apply!

ALL THE FEELS …

- [ ] Calm AF
- [ ] Blind panic
- [ ] Total shit loss
- [ ] It's about time
- [ ] WTAF
- [ ] Healthy rush of nerves
- [ ] I've got this definitely
- [ ] Haven't got this
- [ ] Immediate military mode
- [ ] Denial
- [ ] Ready and prepared
- [ ] Terrified

- [ ] Excited
- [ ] Unprepared
- [ ] Ouch
- [ ] Here we go
- [ ] I need a poo
- [ ] Get me a drink
- [ ] _____
- [ ] _____
- [ ] _____
- [ ] _____
- [ ] _____
- [ ] _____

The Stats

This may not be the traditional baby record book, but you better believe we're here for the all-important stuff too.

Date of birth: Time of birth:

Weight at birth: Sex:

Hair: Yes   No   Colour

Birth place:

Star sign: Birthstone:

Labour:

Time labour started   Where did labour start?

Hours in labour?

Support team:
Doctors, nurses, midwives, donors, surrogates, birth parents, neighbours, the Deliveroo guy … this is a chance to write a human gratitude list to all the people that helped your baby arrive safely.

Name and role

Name and role

Name and role

Name and role

On the Day You Were Born ...

It was a ... (what day of the week?)

Sunrise

Weather

Sunset

UK #1

Most watched TV series

US #1

Celebrities who share your birthday

Must-see film this year

Prime Minister

Monarch

Chinese Year of the

US President

Our address was

The Stats

This may not be the traditional baby record book, but you better believe we're here for the all-important stuff too.

Date of birth: Time of birth:

Weight at birth: Sex:

Hair: Yes   No   Colour

Birth place:

Star sign: Birthstone:

Labour:

Time labour started   Where did labour start?

Hours in labour?

Support team:
Doctors, nurses, midwives, donors, surrogates, birth parents, neighbours, the Deliveroo guy … this is a chance to write a human gratitude list to all the people that helped your baby arrive safely.

Name and role

Name and role

Name and role

Name and role

On the Day You Were Born ...

It was a ... (what day of the week?)

Weather

UK #1

US #1

Must-see film this year

Prime Minister

Monarch

US President

Sunrise

Sunset

Most watched TV series

Celebrities who share your birthday

Chinese Year of the

Our address was

People were wearing

_____

Price of a pint of milk

_____

Average house price

_____

Cost of a first-class stamp

_____

**Stick in the front
page of a favourite
newspaper and keep it
folded here from the
day they were born**

Best Laid Plans

HOW IT STARTED ...

When I gave birth it was called a 'Birth Plan' and, because I'm an idiot, mine was four pages, front and back, laminated and colour-coded. Oh, how the midwives must have had a chuckle at that. Now they've updated it to 'Birth Preferences', which is definitely better but I prefer to call it ...

'The list of stuff I'd like to happen if possible but, to be honest, I'm not that fussed and I'm really only bothered about getting through this with myself, my baby, my mental health and my vulva intact.'

(You may or may not have a vulva, or your vulva may not be the vulva in question ... either way, we should all pray for the vulva.)

PREFERENCES ...

You can write out your preferences here or
stick it in if you have a hard copy.

HOW IT'S GOING ...

Now that we've established what you wanted to happen, let's talk about what actually happened – because this is the stuff that memories are made of and maybe, down the line, dinner party stories.

Performance Review: Birthing Partner

BIRTHING PARTNER INFO

Name:

Relationship to birth-giver:

CHARACTERISTIC	Excellent	Good enough	Will just about do	Woeful
AVAILABILITY: in other words, were they where they needed to be when they needed to be there?				
KNOWLEDGE OF THE 'HOLY SHIT! IT'S HAPPENING!' PLAN: please consider efficiency in getting all necessary things together, getting birth pool ready, if applicable, and/or making it to the hospital drama-free.				
CALM DISPOSITION: consider whether they were able to stay calm but also keep the birth-giver calm.				
BIRTH PREFERENCES: were they fully aware of all preferences, had copies of the birth preferences to hand at all times and were able to communicate these clearly where necessary?				
ESSENTIAL SKILLS: massage, snacks, entertainment, provisions etc.				
MULTI-TASKING: ability to manage all personnel involved both on site and virtually (e.g. doctors/family/friends).				
CONSCIOUSNESS: did they manage to stay awake at all key times?				
POSITIVITY: were they able to maintain a positive mental attitude at all times?				
TACT AND SENSITIVITY: consider ability to not complain in any way, shape or form from the moment you went into labour until the day the child turns 18.				

Gratitude List

There are always lots of people to thank when you become a parent ... however that happens. This is your chance to list all those people and things you were grateful to have with you on your journey to being a parent.

The Name Game

Choosing a name can feel like an insurmountable task at times. Not only do you both have to find a name that you agree on (if there's two of you) when you can barely agree on what kind of takeaway to get on a Friday night, but you'll probably have to put up with Great Aunty Doris saying she wants you to give it a 'proper name'. Here's my advice: You do you. No explanations. No apologies.

BabyNameGoesHere

NAMES WE CONSIDERED

Girl

Boy

Your Actual Name

Write your baby's name below and decorate it however you wish.

Why we chose it ...

WHAT WE ENDED UP CALLING YOU

What cute nicknames did you find yourself calling your baby? Crotch goblin? Vagina fruit? Tiny Terrorist? You can keep adding to this over the years.

Instagram vs. Reality

The 'real' first picture of you
and your baby post-birth.

The picture you posted to Instagram
and texted to friends and family to
announce the birth of your baby.

Talking of Photos ...

I wish I'd spent more time thinking about the photos I wanted to take in those first few hours, days and weeks. I was so bloody knackered it didn't even cross my mind. As it turns out, I wasn't the only one who felt like this. My good friend, photographer and mum to three, Charlotte Gray, felt the same way and created a checklist of photos to help new parents capture those magical moments forever. Charlotte says:

@charlotte grayphotography

Taking photographs is probably not high on the priority list when you've just given birth, but the lack of photos following the births of my three children is something I really regret. This list is designed to act as a prompt or reminder to get a couple of photographs when you have a moment.

Don't worry about perfection. Don't worry about make-up. Just raw, natural photos of your new baby with you and your partner, and the amazing chaos that now surrounds you. Your aim is to tell a story. Your photos don't have to be shot in chronological order – someone in labour will not appreciate you stopping to take a photo of the outside of the hospital when all they want to do is get to the labour ward! Just capture as much as you can, when the time is right, and you can sequence the images later.

There are two lists here – one for hospital and one for home-birth. If you have a hospital birth, once home make sure to get photographs of all or both of you together. You can buy camera phone tripods and remotes very reasonably online. A remote will mean you can take the photo without having to run to get in the shot.

HOSPITAL/BIRTHING UNIT

- Outside of hospital

- Room number

- Curtain view – looking into the room or cubicle with the curtain in the foreground.

- Baby being checked and/or weighed (this doesn't have to be the moment they are born – other checks will be made and you can ask medical staff if they mind you taking photos of the baby whilst they check her/him).

- Wrist bands on mum and baby

- Mum and baby in bed

- Skin to skin

- Feeding the baby

- Parents changing the baby on the bed.

- Hospital bassinette – photograph the baby from above (and through the side, if perspex).

- Going home outfit

- If there is something in your room that relates to the baby, take a shot of it.

HOME BIRTH

- Your midwife team (if they are happy to be in a photo)

- A wide shot of the room

- Skin to skin

- Checking and weighing the baby

- Mum and baby tucked up in bed afterwards

- Baby's first change

- Baby's first outfit

- Feeding the baby

The Village

There's no such thing as a 'normal' family and so I didn't want to include a family tree. These days we build our own villages to help us raise our children. Whether it's friends, family, instamates, neighbours or the dog ... here's a chance to celebrate them all.

Name:

Relationship:

One word to describe them:

Name:

Relationship:

One word to describe them:

Name:

Relationship:

One word to describe them:

Name:

Relationship:

One word to describe them:

Name:

Relationship:

One word to describe them:

Name:

Relationship:

One word to describe them:

Name:

Relationship:

One word to describe them:

Name:

Relationship:

One word to describe them:

Name:

Relationship:

One word to describe them:

Name:

Relationship:

One word to describe them:

Name:

Relationship:

One word to describe them:

Name:

Relationship:

One word to describe them:

Making Your Mark

I know your baby may feel massive – especially if you've just had to pass a baby-shaped camel through the eye of a vulva-sized needle – but trust me, you'll forget just how small they are. Use this space to pop in a handprint and a footprint. Sorry in advance for all the mess.

Top Advice

This parenting lark is hard and there's no way you can be expected to do it all on your own. Whatever your set up, there will hopefully be people you can lean on when you need them. Hopefully they'll turn into people your kid can lean on later in life, too. So, in preparation for that, ask those closest to you to put their one piece of advice here for your kid to look back on later in life and learn from.

NAME	MY ADVICE TO YOU IS ...

3

New Kid on the Block

(the First 12 Months)

Friend:
'My new puppy is just like having a baby!'

Me:
'Does that puppy chew on your nipples until they bleed?'

Monthly Memories

It's not easy to remember much about the early months. Having a baby is a bit like watching a bomb explode in your house, over and over, every day until they move out. Plus, you're so incredibly sleep deprived that you struggle to remember what day of the week it is, never mind the little memory-making minutiae that you want to be able to remind them of for the rest of their life. This is where you can record all that stuff. Two things to remember:

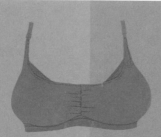

You love it when

You hate it when

Things you nailed this month

Your favourite toy

Firsts this month

Your favourite place to sleep

Your favourite game to play

The funniest thing you did this month

It makes you smile when

Our favourite thing to do

It makes you cry when

Weight   Eye colour   Hair colour

Month 2

Things I nailed this month

_____

_____

My most impressive parenting
fail this month

_____

Things I did this month that I never
thought I'd do (but here we are)

_____

_____

Things I was not expecting this month

_____

_____

The easiest thing this month

_____

The hardest thing this month

_____

I introduced you to these people

_____

_____

My favourite moment this month

_____

_____

I could not have survived this month
without

_____

One word to describe this month

_____

One person I'd like to thank this month:

_____

One thing I learned this month

_____

Next month I want to

_____

_____

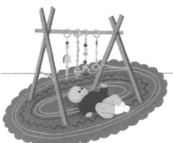

You love it when

_____

You hate it when

_____

Things you nailed this month

_____

Your favourite toy

_____

_____

Firsts this month

Your favourite place to sleep

_____

_____

Your favourite game to play

_____

The funniest thing you did this month

_____

It makes you smile when

_____

_____

Our favourite thing to do

It makes you cry when

_____

_____

Weight   Eye colour   Hair colour

_____

Month 3

Things I nailed this month

_____

_____

My most impressive parenting
fail this month

_____

Things I did this month that I never
thought I'd do (but here we are)

_____

_____

Things I was not expecting this month

_____

_____

The easiest thing this month

_____

The hardest thing this month

_____

I introduced you to these people

_____

_____

My favourite moment this month

_____

_____

I could not have survived this month
without

_____

One word to describe this month

_____

One person I'd like to thank this month:

_____

One thing I learned this month

_____

Next month I want to

_____

_____

Baby

You love it when
_____

You hate it when
_____

Things you nailed this month
_____

_____

Your favourite toy
_____

Firsts this month
_____

Your favourite place to sleep
_____

_____

Your favourite game to play
_____

The funniest thing you did this month
_____

It makes you smile when
_____

_____

Our favourite thing to do
_____

It makes you cry when
_____

Weight   Eye colour   Hair colour

_____   _____   _____

Month 4

Parent

Things I nailed this month

_____

_____

My most impressive parenting
fail this month

_____

Things I did this month that I never
thought I'd do (but here we are)

_____

_____

Things I was not expecting this month

_____

_____

The easiest thing this month

_____

The hardest thing this month

_____

I introduced you to these people

_____

_____

My favourite moment this month

_____

_____

I could not have survived this month
without

_____

One word to describe this month

_____

One person I'd like to thank this month:

_____

One thing I learned this month

_____

Next month I want to

_____

_____

Things you nailed this month

Firsts this month

The funniest thing you did this month

Our favourite thing to do

You love it when

You hate it when

Your favourite toy

Your favourite place to sleep

Your favourite game to play

It makes you smile when

It makes you cry when

Weight

Eye colour

Hair colour

Month 5

Things I nailed this month

I introduced you to these people

My most impressive parenting
fail this month

My favourite moment this month

Things I did this month that I never
thought I'd do (but here we are)

I could not have survived this month
without

One word to describe this month

Things I was not expecting this month

One person I'd like to thank this month:

The easiest thing this month

One thing I learned this month

The hardest thing this month

Next month I want to

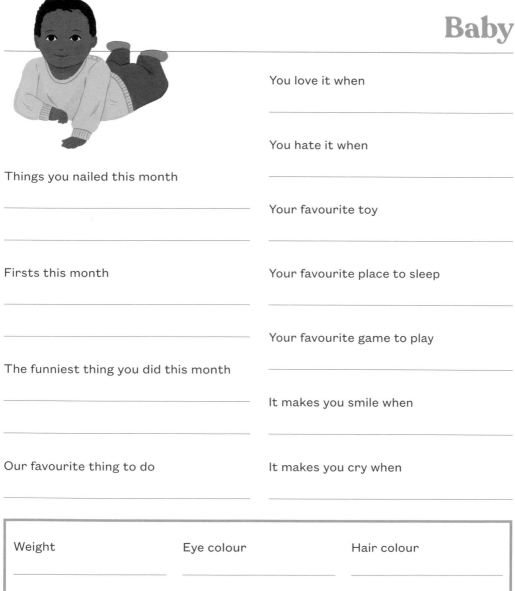

Baby

Things you nailed this month

Firsts this month

The funniest thing you did this month

Our favourite thing to do

You love it when

You hate it when

Your favourite toy

Your favourite place to sleep

Your favourite game to play

It makes you smile when

It makes you cry when

Weight

Eye colour

Hair colour

Month 6

Parent

Things I nailed this month

_____

_____

My most impressive parenting
fail this month

_____

Things I did this month that I never
thought I'd do (but here we are)

_____

_____

Things I was not expecting this month

_____

_____

The easiest thing this month

_____

The hardest thing this month

_____

I introduced you to these people

_____

_____

My favourite moment this month

_____

_____

I could not have survived this month
without

_____

One word to describe this month

_____

One person I'd like to thank this month:

_____

One thing I learned this month

_____

Next month I want to

_____

_____

Baby

You love it when

You hate it when

Things you nailed this month

Your favourite toy

Firsts this month

Your favourite place to sleep

Your favourite game to play

The funniest thing you did this month

It makes you smile when

Our favourite thing to do

It makes you cry when

Weight   Eye colour   Hair colour

Month 7

Things I nailed this month

_____

_____

My most impressive parenting
fail this month

_____

Things I did this month that I never
thought I'd do (but here we are)

_____

_____

Things I was not expecting this month

_____

_____

The easiest thing this month

_____

The hardest thing this month

_____

I introduced you to these people

_____

_____

My favourite moment this month

_____

_____

I could not have survived this month
without

_____

One word to describe this month

_____

One person I'd like to thank this month:

_____

One thing I learned this month

_____

Next month I want to

_____

_____

Baby

Things you nailed this month

_____

_____

Firsts this month

_____

_____

The funniest thing you did this month

_____

_____

Our favourite thing to do

_____

You love it when

_____

You hate it when

_____

Your favourite toy

_____

Your favourite place to sleep

_____

Your favourite game to play

_____

It makes you smile when

_____

It makes you cry when

_____

Weight	Eye colour	Hair colour
_____	_____	_____

Month 8

Things I nailed this month

_____

_____

My most impressive parenting
fail this month

_____

Things I did this month that I never
thought I'd do (but here we are)

_____

_____

Things I was not expecting this month

_____

_____

The easiest thing this month

_____

The hardest thing this month

_____

I introduced you to these people

_____

_____

My favourite moment this month

_____

_____

I could not have survived this month
without

_____

One word to describe this month

_____

One person I'd like to thank this month:

_____

One thing I learned this month

_____

Next month I want to

_____

_____

Baby

You love it when

You hate it when

Things you nailed this month

Your favourite toy

Firsts this month

Your favourite place to sleep

Your favourite game to play

The funniest thing you did this month

It makes you smile when

Our favourite thing to do

It makes you cry when

Weight	Eye colour	Hair colour

Month 9

Things I nailed this month

_____

_____

My most impressive parenting
fail this month

_____

Things I did this month that I never
thought I'd do (but here we are)

_____

_____

Things I was not expecting this month

_____

_____

The easiest thing this month

_____

The hardest thing this month

_____

I introduced you to these people

_____

_____

My favourite moment this month

_____

_____

I could not have survived this month
without

_____

One word to describe this month

_____

One person I'd like to thank this month:

_____

One thing I learned this month

_____

Next month I want to

_____

_____

Baby

Things you nailed this month

_____

_____

Firsts this month

_____

_____

The funniest thing you did this month

_____

_____

Our favourite thing to do

_____

You love it when

_____

You hate it when

_____

Your favourite toy

_____

Your favourite place to sleep

_____

Your favourite game to play

_____

It makes you smile when

_____

It makes you cry when

_____

Weight

_____

Eye colour

_____

Hair colour

_____

Month 10

Things I nailed this month

_____

_____

I introduced you to these people

_____

_____

My most impressive parenting
fail this month

_____

My favourite moment this month

_____

_____

Things I did this month that I never
thought I'd do (but here we are)

_____

_____

I could not have survived this month
without

_____

One word to describe this month

_____

Things I was not expecting this month

_____

_____

One person I'd like to thank this month:

_____

The easiest thing this month

_____

One thing I learned this month

_____

The hardest thing this month

_____

Next month I want to

_____

_____

Baby

Things you nailed this month

Firsts this month

The funniest thing you did this month

Our favourite thing to do

You love it when

You hate it when

Your favourite toy

Your favourite place to sleep

Your favourite game to play

It makes you smile when

It makes you cry when

Weight

Eye colour

Hair colour

Month 11

Things I nailed this month

_____

_____

My most impressive parenting
fail this month

_____

Things I did this month that I never
thought I'd do (but here we are)

_____

_____

Things I was not expecting this month

_____

_____

The easiest thing this month

_____

The hardest thing this month

_____

I introduced you to these people

_____

_____

My favourite moment this month

_____

_____

I could not have survived this month
without

_____

One word to describe this month

_____

One person I'd like to thank this month:

_____

One thing I learned this month

_____

Next month I want to

_____

_____

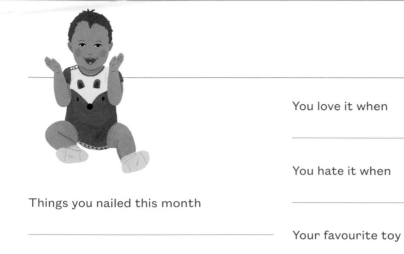

Baby

Things you nailed this month

_____

_____

Firsts this month

_____

_____

The funniest thing you did this month

_____

_____

Our favourite thing to do

_____

You love it when

_____

You hate it when

_____

Your favourite toy

_____

Your favourite place to sleep

_____

Your favourite game to play

_____

It makes you smile when

_____

It makes you cry when

_____

Weight	Eye colour	Hair colour
_____	_____	_____

Month 12

Things I nailed this month

_____

_____

My most impressive parenting
fail this month

_____

Things I did this month that I never
thought I'd do (but here we are)

_____

_____

Things I was not expecting this month

_____

_____

The easiest thing this month

_____

The hardest thing this month

_____

I introduced you to these people

_____

_____

My favourite moment this month

_____

_____

I could not have survived this month
without

_____

One word to describe this month

_____

One person I'd like to thank this month:

_____

One thing I learned this month

_____

Next month I want to

_____

_____

Baby

Things you nailed this month

_____

_____

Firsts this month

_____

_____

The funniest thing you did this month

_____

_____

Our favourite thing to do

_____

You love it when

_____

You hate it when

_____

Your favourite toy

_____

Your favourite place to sleep

_____

Your favourite game to play

_____

It makes you smile when

_____

It makes you cry when

_____

Weight   Eye colour   Hair colour

_____   _____   _____

The First Year: Customer Review

Woohoo! You made it. You've completed your first year as a parent *insert happy dance here ... if you've got the energy, of course. While there aren't any medals winging their way to you (trust me, there bloody should be), I want you to know that you are your baby's favourite person in the whole wide world, which means you must be doing a lot of things right.

It's been an adventure (read: absolute headf*ck of the most gargantuan proportions). You'll have found some things incredibly easy. Some things will have reduced you and everyone you live with to tears. You'll have wondered why you ever thought having a baby was a good idea, while at the same time, wondering how you ever lived without your little crying, stinky, snuggly bundle of joy.

With that being said, here's your chance to review your baby ... because that's a totally normal thing to do.

DATE:

How happy are you with your baby?

Was your baby delivered in a timely manner?

Does your experience of your baby fit the description given pre-birth?

Is your baby value for sleep loss?

How likely are you to recommend this experience to a friend?

Your First Birthday

My feelings on your first birthday.

Your First Birthday

Use this spread to capture the spirit of the big day! Stick photos, note down what presents you received or add a new handprint – whatever you want!

From Me to You ...

Writing letters to your children as they grow has been one of my favourite parenting things. It's a great idea to set up an email account for them and write to them there whenever you want to.

You can hand the account over to them as soon as they are old enough. In the meantime, here's a chance to write a letter to your baby after year one.

4

Milestones

(Up to 2 years old)

'You spend the first 2 years wishing, praying and hoping they'll start talking. Then you spend the next 30 wishing they'd shut up.'

The Things Kids Do

It's always tricky talking about milestones because all babies are different and they do things at different times. My first baby walked at 11 months but I suspect that was because she was built like a Minecraft character and far too chunky to be able to haul herself around crawling. My second baby didn't walk until she was 17 months and she hasn't sat still since.

With that in mind, I've decided to put all the 'firsts' here, which you can date yourself, rather than organise them by date. What one baby can do in the first month can take another baby two or three to master. The last thing I want this book to do is send you into a spiral of worry because your little one hasn't figured out their elbow from their butthole yet.

First smile

Date:

First giggle

Date:

First exploding nappy

Date:

First roll over

Date:

First bath

Date:

First puke

Date:

First sit up

Date:

First crawl/shuffle

Date:

First grab for something

Date:

First pull to stand up

Date:

First free stand

Date:

First steps

Date:

First full night's sleep (note: this could take years)

Date:

_____

First food

Date:

What was it?

_____

First time you drank from a cup

Date:

_____

First word

Date:

And the word was

_____

First time you said 'mama'

Date:

_____

First time you said 'dada'

Date:

_____

First sentence

Date:

Your first sentence was

_____

First time you said your own name

Date:

How you pronounced it

_____

First time on a plane

Date:

_____

First tooth

Date:

_____

First time on the beach

Date:

_____

First pair of shoes

Date:

_____

First haircut

Date:

_____

First holiday

Date:

Where?

_____

First song you sang

Date:

What was it?

_____

First dance

Date:

_____

First day at childcare

Date:

Where?

_____

First meal at a restaurant

Date:

Where?

_____

First friend

_____

First poo in the bath

Date:

_____

Any other firsts?

_____

_____

_____

_____

_____

Other Stuff

Other hilarious/terrifying/amazing/shocking stuff your little bundle of joy did that's worth remembering.

DATE	WHAT HAPPENED

Parenting Firsts

First time you remembered to take everything with you when you left the house

Date:

_____

First time you Googled 'How to get my baby to sleep through the night'

Date:

_____

First full night's sleep

Date:

_____

First time you panic-bought something that you later regretted and/or never used

Date:

_____

First time without the baby

Date:

_____

First time you picked your child's nose

Date:

_____

First date night

Date:

_____

First post-baby shag

Date:

_____

First hangover

Date:

_____

First night out with friends

Date:

_____

First time you wore something other than leggings or trackies post-birth

Date:

_____

First time you had a fight with your partner over who was more tired

Date:

First time you took your baby away overnight

Date:

Where did you go?

First time you wore make-up post-birth

Date:

First time you went away without your baby

Date:

First time you gave something sour to your baby to watch their reaction

Date:

_____

First time you exercised post-birth

Date:

_____

First time you went to the supermarket on your own

Date:

_____

First lie you told your child

Date:

What was it?

_____

First mum-friend you made

Name:

Where did you meet?

_____

First time you had to catch
puke in your hands

Date:

Where were you?

_____

First time you cleaned yourself with
baby wipes

Date:

_____

First time you and your partner cried
because it was so hard

Date:

_____

First time someone asked you when
you're having the next one

Date:

_____

First time you thought you lost them in
a public place

Date:

Where were you?

_____

First time you found a poo not in a toilet
or a nappy

Date:

Where was it?

_____

Parenting Wins

Other parenting firsts/wins/hacks that you don't want to forget.

DATE	WHAT HAPPENED

5

High Five!

(Years 2-5)

'You're going to really want to remember the love and joy you felt when that baby arrived, because now you're about to discover that they've scribbled on the walls with a Sharpie and cut themselves a fringe.'

My mum, on my daughter's second birthday.

Some Unsolicited Advice That You Didn't Ask For ...

Remember when you were struggling with adjusting to having a baby and people told you that, 'This too shall pass'? Well, I've got good news and bad news. The good news is that they were right. The baby phase has officially passed. The bad news? Welcome to the 'terrible twos', the 'threenados' and the 'four-fuls'.

Sure, there are some amazing moments over the next three years that you are really going to cherish, but you're going to want to write those down as evidence because, in my experience, the only things I can remember about those years are the times they made me want to pull my fingernails off in frustration. (But don't worry – your little angel probably won't do any of these things.)

The time my daughter cut her hair, her best friend's hair, my Egyptian cotton bedsheets and her friend's NASA t-shirt that he was sent from the States.

The time I found my daughters 'adventuring' on to the extension roof via their bedroom window at 9pm and throwing stones at the neighbour's roof.

The time my daughter wrote a story on the wall with a Sharpie pen. The story sucked.

The time my daughter played with my make-up and managed to destroy a couple of hundred quid's worth and the rug in the process.

The time I took her on a night flight from Denver, Colorado to London by myself and she screamed the whole way home.

That being said, there are some pretty amazing things about this age ... like when they finally learn to wipe their own butt, feed themselves without decorating the kitchen wall and floors and, of course, walk without falling over nothing and bumping into everything.

They're also developing their own buzzing, creative, stubborn and totally illogical little brains, meaning that they're also about to cotton on to the fact that they can make their own decisions. So ... yeah, good luck with that. And to help you remember all these wonderful things, we're kicking off with a list of their favourite things.

Playing Favourites

Favourite TV show

_____

Favourite parent (Joke! ... But really?)

_____

Favourite activity

_____

Favourite breakfast

_____

Favourite lunch

_____

Favourite dinner

_____

AT 2 YEARS OLD

Favourite snack

_____

Favourite toy

_____

Favourite drink

_____

Favourite game

_____

Favourite colour

_____

Favourite film

_____

Favourite animal

_____

Favourite song

_____

Favourite superhero

_____

Favourite fruit

_____

Favourite ice cream flavour

_____

Favourite place in the house

_____

Favourite place outside

_____

Favourite friend

_____

Favourite place to nap

_____

Favourite outfit

_____

Favourite book

_____

Favourite word

_____

AT 3 YEARS OLD

Favourite toy

_____

Favourite game

_____

Favourite film

_____

Favourite song

_____

Favourite colour

Favourite animal

Favourite superhero

Favourite fruit

Favourite TV show

Favourite ice cream flavour

Favourite parent (Joke! ... But really?)

Favourite place in the house

Favourite activity

Favourite place outside

Favourite breakfast

Favourite friend

Favourite lunch

Favourite place to nap

Favourite dinner

Favourite outfit

Favourite snack

Favourite book

Favourite drink

Favourite word

AT 4 YEARS OLD

Favourite toy

Favourite game

Favourite film

Favourite song

Favourite TV show

Favourite parent (Joke! ... But really?)

Favourite activity

Favourite breakfast

Favourite lunch

Favourite dinner

Favourite snack

Favourite drink

Favourite colour

Favourite animal

Favourite superhero

Favourite fruit

_____

Favourite ice cream flavour

_____

Favourite place in the house

_____

Favourite place outside

_____

Favourite friend

_____

Favourite place to nap

_____

Favourite outfit

_____

Favourite book

_____

Favourite word

_____

AT 5 YEARS OLD

Favourite toy

_____

Favourite game

_____

Favourite film

_____

Favourite song

_____

Favourite TV show

_____

Favourite parent (Joke! ... But really?)

_____

Favourite activity

_____

Favourite breakfast

_____

Favourite lunch

_____

Favourite dinner

_____

Favourite snack

_____

Favourite drink

_____

Favourite colour

_____

Favourite animal

_____

Favourite superhero

_____

Favourite fruit

_____

Favourite ice cream flavour

_____

Favourite place in the house

_____

Favourite place outside

_____

Favourite friend

_____

Favourite place to nap

_____

Favourite outfit

_____

Favourite book

_____

Favourite word

_____

Cool Stuff Kids Learn

As your child goes through toddlerhood, the stuff they start to learn is mind blowing. Of course, all kids do things at different times, so please don't let Janet down the road make you feel bad because her child is singing 'Silent Night' in Mandarin while folding origami hedgehogs, whipping up a stir-fry and riding a penny farthing. These are in no particular order.

ON THIS DAY YOU ...

Said the alphabet from A–Z

_____

Wrote your name for the first time

_____

Counted to 10

_____

Counted to 20

_____

Tied your first shoe-lace

_____

Rode a bike without stabilisers

_____

Read your first book

_____

Spelled your first word

_____

Used a cup

_____

Used a knife and fork

_____

Caught a ball

_____

Did a roly-poly

_____

Swam without a flotation aid

_____

Ate a meal without knocking over
your drink

_____

Sang the words to a song that wasn't a
nursery rhyme

_____

First Days

Of course, we love our kids; we want to hold them close and never let them go … but we also want to be able to go for a wee on our own, clean the house and have it stay that way, finish a hot drink

DAYCARE

Your first day at nursery was

_____

The nursery you went to was

_____

You felt …………on your first day

_____

I felt …………on your first day

_____

Your key worker was

_____

in one sitting without having to put it in the microwave and maybe watch some trashy TV that doesn't involve oversized, anthropomorphised animals being bratty. Yes, Bing! I'm looking at you.

So, this section is all about the places we send them so that other people can look after them and teach them important stuff.

PRIMARY SCHOOL

Your first day at primary school was

I felt............on your first day

The primary school you went to was

Your first teacher was

You felt............on your first day

Parent Bingo

It is a truth universally acknowledged that a parent in possession of a child to raise will, despite all efforts to the contrary, end up sounding like their own parents. Don't bother resisting it – save that energy for getting through the sleepless nights – it's going to happen. Before you know it, certain phrases you swore you would never utter come flying out of your mouth, so let's have fun with it!

Parents, I introduce to you … Parent Bingo. Simply cross them off as soon as you hear yourself saying them.

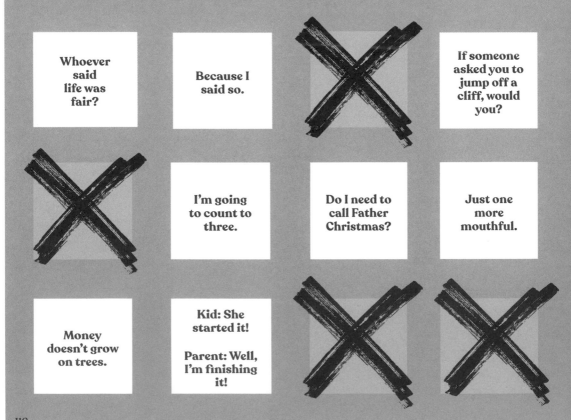

Whoever said life was fair?	Because I said so.	✗	If someone asked you to jump off a cliff, would you?
✗	I'm going to count to three.	Do I need to call Father Christmas?	Just one more mouthful.
Money doesn't grow on trees.	Kid: She started it! Parent: Well, I'm finishing it!	✗	✗

What did
your last
slave die of?

You'll take
someone's
eye out with
that.

You'll get
square eyes.

It'll all end in
tears.

I want, never
gets.

Were you
born in a
barn?

There's no
such word
as can't.

Only boring
people get
bored.

Who is 'she'?
The cat's
mother?

You'll live.

Not under
my roof.

Don't make
me pull this
car over.

Now We Are 5

How EVER you got here, be proud that you made it! Your kid is now five, probably in school, and you've probably found your feet as you stand in the scariest hood of all: parenthood. It's time to write a letter again, to your 5-year-old.

6

Just a Note

'They say it takes a village to raise a kid.
Could someone send me the directions
to that village please and thank you?'

Before I leave you to embark on the rest of your parenting life,

I wanted to take this chance to tell you something I wish I'd learned a lot earlier on than I did. The irony of what I'm about to say is not lost on me, but here goes: throw away all the books that tell you they know more than you about being a parent.

We've gotten used to quietening our instincts and ignoring our gut when it comes to parenting. I don't know about you but when I was fretting (read: going out of my tiny mind) about something I should or shouldn't be doing as a parent, 9 times out of 10, I already knew the answer. Ok, maybe not the 'answer', but I knew what felt like the right thing to try. In the beginning, I often ignored that and nearly killed myself trying to follow someone else's advice because, hey, they had a whole book. Surely, they were the expert?

No. When it comes to your baby or child, you are the expert. It doesn't matter whether you've birthed them yourself or not – that's just logistics. You know yourself better than anyone else and you know your child better than anyone else; harness that knowledge and use it. Sure, listen to advice, ask questions, do research, but, in the end, any decision you make should be yours.

That confidence isn't easy to come by and the current messaging in parenting does very little to support its growth, but I'm telling you – you really do know what's best for you and your child and screw what anyone else thinks.

Some good news: it's actually quite hard to mess up parenting beyond repair. You really have to be committed to being a crappy parent over a considerable amount of time for you to even come close to winning the 'Worst Parent in the World' award – so, cut yourself some slack. You're going to fuck up, you'll make gargantuan, soul-crippling mistakes. You'll lose your temper, you'll scream empty threats, you'll cry, you'll slam doors, you'll say things you don't mean and you'll hate yourself for it but, please, learn to forgive yourself and remember that it's all about the repair.

Be the parent that says sorry. Model that shit. Show them how it's done. Mess up and make it right. It's one of the best things we can teach our kids: accountability.

With that … I'm out of here. My kids are literally going to tear the house down while I write this book and I'm about to tear my hair out. They're 5 and 8 before you ask so, yeah, it's still carnage at this stage too.

Sending strength and solidarity. May the sleeps be long and the tantrums short.

Peace.

Cat
x

Acknowledgements

The fact that I even have the chance to write these acknowledgements at the back of a book that I created still blows my mind. There are so many people to say thank you to, so I'm just going to get on with it.

I have to lead by thanking my wonderful agent, Bonnie Barry. Friend and fellow mum, both of us just trying to make our way in a world that for a long time we didn't believe was going to make room for us. You came into my life when I was at my lowest professionally, there was a pandemic, lockdown, home-schooling and a metric fuck tonne of anxiety but you took me on and made magic happen – look at us now babe! You still make that magic happen every day and I'm bloody lucky to have you by my side.

To the whole team at HarperCollins for believing that I was the right person to write this book. I don't think you'll ever know how much it meant to me – although you probably guessed when I cried tears of joyful disbelief in the meeting. To Anna Mrowiec for being the best editor ever and putting up with my constant panicked emails! You were incredibly patient with me and never made me feel stupid or annoying so for that, I truly thank you. Thanks also to Sim Greenaway for the gorgeous design, George Atsiaris and Julia Pollacco from the editorial team and Alan Cracknell from production for all your hard work on it.

If you've spent the whole time working through this book thinking, 'Yeah, I mean the book's ok but the illustrations are just out of this world,' then I don't blame you! Thank you to the unbelievably talented Maja Tomljanovic who brought the whole book to life. I hope that whoever you are and wherever you are, you were able to see yourself at some point.

To my closest girlfriends who have done nothing but cheer me on and build me up: Reagan Kempton, Anna Hristou, Anna Whitehouse, Natalie Lee, Cherry Healey and the wonderful Charlotte Gray whose photography skills defy every sleepless night and early morning that can be plainly seen on my face. To the Glorious Bitches – you know who you are – the guinea pig memes are what keep me sane. To my sister, Samantha Sweet, who introduced me to the universe and told me to ask it for what I wanted – I normally hate it when you're right but on this occasion I'm glad you were.

To my mum and dad. Dad, I love that every time we speak, you ask me proudly how many followers I've got on Instagram now, even though we both know you have no idea what I actually do on there! You gave me a love for the written word and for that I'll always be grateful. And to my mum: I see now what you did for me as a mother and what you gave up every day to make sure I had every opportunity and experience. Thank you doesn't quite seem enough but it's all I have.

And of course, thank you Team Sims: Jimmy Sims, Billie and Bo. Jimmy, thank you for all the bedtimes you did while I hid in the office with my headphones on putting this together, and for brainstorming with me when I'd run out of 'funny'. I'm not sure what I did to get this lucky but you are the introvert to my extrovert, the quiet to my loud, the considered to my impulsive. I don't know why it works so well, but it really does. I love you. To Billie and Bo – you truly are the most wonderful ratbags. The dirty laughs, the funny accents, the 'sky-cuddles', the kitchen dance parties, the morning snuggles, the tickles, the times

you slip your little hands into mine, the shade you throw, the jokes you make up … you're a lot but I wouldn't want any less and don't let anyone ever make you feel like you need to be smaller than you are. While I'm proud of this book I made, you guys will always remain my greatest creation. Thank you to Noodle and Jazz for the cuddles along the way as well.

Finally, if you've followed me and supported me on Instagram then you get the biggest shout out of all. I don't take a single one of you for granted. All of this is only because you've followed, liked, shared, laughed and told your mates. It all began when I was a new mum, totally lost, mentally and emotionally paralysed, broken and wondering what the fuck I'd done. It was a time when I thought becoming a mum had taken my world away. Now I realise that it was only just beginning. I'm here for each and every one of you.

Where to Find Support

I'm going to go ahead and assume that you are deeply in love with your children, but I'm not going to assume that you are loving the job of parenting. The two things can be true at the same time. It's hard. Really hard. Trust me, I've got the 'Becoming a parent nearly broke me' t-shirt and wear it daily. This is a list of a few organisations, charities and individuals who are there to help you whenever you need it.

Social Media and in Real Life Communities for Parents

- **Mothers Meeting**
  Founded by Jenny Scott, Mothers Meeting is all about bringing mums together in a cool and fresh way. There are IRL meet ups as well as a huge online community.
  @mothersmeeting
  www.mothersmeeting.com
- **Mums That Rave**
  An award-winning community organising IRL raves and panel events to help empower and inspire mums.
  @mumsthatrave
  www.mumsthatrave.com
- **Peanut and Mush**
  Online apps offering online 'dating' sites for parents who want to make connections with other parents in their area.
  @peanut @mushmums
- **The MotherMind Way**
  Founded by psychotherapist and author, Anna Mathur, The MotherMind Way is a hub to help you enjoy a happier motherhood with therapeutic resources.
  @themothermindway
- **The Mum Club**
  An online community connecting women who happen to have children.
  @themumclub

Maternal Mental Health

- **The Maternal Mental Health Alliance**
  www.maternalmentalhealthalliance.org
  info@maternalmentalhealthalliance.org
- **PaNDAS: PND Awareness and Support**
  www.pandasfoundation.org
  0808 1961 776
- **MumsAid: Supporting Mums and Their Families**
  www.mums-aid.org
  info@mums-aid.org
  07758 763908
- **Mothers for Mothers: Postnatal Mental Health Support**
  www.mothersformothers.co.uk
  support@mothersformothers.co.uk
  0117 9359366

- APNI: Association for Post Natal Illness
www.apni.org
info@apni.org
0207 386 0868

Support for Dads

- Dads Matter UK
www.dadsmatteruk.org
- Daddilife
www.daddilife.com
- Dad Info
www.dad.info
info@dad.info

Adoption

- We Are Family: Adoption Support Community
www.wearefamilyadoption.org.uk
hello@wearefamilyadoption.org.uk
- Adoption UK
www.adoptionuk.org
0300 666 0006

Multiple Births

- Twins and Multiples
Twins Trust
www.twinstrust.org
enquiries@twinstrust.org
01252 332 344
- The Multiple Births Foundation
www.multiplebirths.org.uk
mbf@bcu.ac.uk
07360 735050

Lone Parenting

- Gingerbread
www.gingerbread.org.uk
0808 802 0925
- Only Dads
www.onlydads.org
info@onlydads.org
- Only Mums
www.onlymums.org
info@onlymums.org

Working Parents

- The Working Parent
www.theworkingparent.com
info@workingparent.com

Family Support

- Home Start
www.home-start.org.uk
info@home-start.org.uk
0116 464 5490

General Mental Health and Crises

- SHOUT
www.giveusashout.org
Text SHOUT to 85258
- Samaritans
www.samaritans.org
jo@samaritans.org
116 123

About the Author

Cat Sims is a content creator, podcaster and now, author who is still trying to figure the whole 'adulting' thing out.

She's made a living out of documenting her failures and successes as a 40-year-old woman, a mother and a wife across various social media platforms.

Her mission in life is to make as many women as possible feel 'seen' and to make them realise that they are never, ever, 'the only one'.

She's honest AF, wonderfully self-deprecating and willing to say all the things the rest of us hide away and, in doing so, manages to make us all feel a little bit better about our perfectly messy lives.

She lives in London with her husband Jimmy Sims, her two girls Billie and Bo, her sausage dog Noodle and her Siamese cat Jazz (and if her laundry is anything to go by, a few hundred other people that she's never met).